W9-ANZ-576

Fatima

by Frederick Lipp

Illustrated by Margaret Sanfilippo Lindmark

*F*atima pinched two fingers around the strands of hair falling over her face and quickly tucked the hair behind her ear. *Sometimes my name makes me feel different*, Fatima thought, as she studied herself in the mirror.

Fatima had learned to answer slowly when people asked her name. She pronounced each syllable: "Fah-TEE-mah." But Fatima's distinctive name didn't prevent her from sharing books with Alice, jumping rope with Mary, or playing math games with Tomás. In fact, Fatima fit in perfectly at school.

Each day when Fatima came home, her mother would inquire, "What did you do at school today?"

Fatima was always happy to share the latest book she had read and discuss art projects and spelling competitions. Fatima would even remember to tell her mother about lunch, especially when it was her favorite—pizza.

Then one day something changed. When Fatima got home, her mother asked, "What did you do at school today?"

"Nothing."

"Nothing? How could that be?" her mother wondered with an arched eyebrow.

"I don't want to talk about it!" Fatima blurted out.

Fatima's mother nodded and asked no further questions. Looking unusually downhearted, Fatima inched her way toward her bedroom. She sat on the corner of her bed, her feet dangling over the edge. As her cat watched from its perch on the windowsill, Fatima hugged her pillow and brooded.

Later that evening, Fatima's mother came into her room and sat beside her. "We need to discuss this," she said. "It's not like you to say that nothing happened after a day at school. Is there anything you would like to talk about?"

"It's just—it's what Billy said," Fatima whispered, her eyes glistening with tears.

"And what did Billy say?" Fatima's mother asked, grasping her hand.

"Billy said he saw us at the grocery store, and that you dress weird—that—that you cover yourself all over and wrap your head in a scarf. He said it looks sort of suspicious and scary. He wonders if you are hiding because maybe you did something wrong." Fatima began to sob. "It's not fair! I told him you're beautiful."

Fatima's mother smiled wistfully and held Fatima close. The cat leapt into Fatima's lap and began purring. For a long time, nothing was said. Fatima rested her head against her mother's shoulder, while the comforting sound of the purring cat filled the uneasy silence. Finally Fatima's mother spoke softly.

"I was taught that the way I dress is a part of our religion, Islam. When I wear the scarf—called the Hijab—and a long dress, I do it so people can see only my face and hands."

"Why?" asked Fatima.

"Because it's not what I look like that matters," her mother replied. "I want people to focus on who I am and what I do. Does it really matter whether I have black or blonde hair?"

Fatima shook her head.

"Right, Fatima—it doesn't matter what I look like. What counts is what I say and then do."

Although Fatima had heard her mother say all of this before, she felt like she was hearing it for the first time. No one had ever made disparaging comments like that about her mother's appearance. Billy had done so simply because she wore a long dress and a scarf that covered her hair and neck.

Fatima kept repeating her mother's words to herself. *"When I speak, it's not what I look like that counts, but what I say and then do…it's not what I look like that counts, but what I say and then do."*

That night as she lay in bed, Fatima devised a plan. She would try to teach Billy and the others in her class that the way a person dresses or looks is not what's important. What really matters is what a person says and then does in life.

The next day at school would be Talk Time. Every Friday, half an hour before school ended, Fatima's teacher encouraged the students in his class to share things that were going on in their lives. Students were asked to write a few notes on a sheet of paper as a reminder of what they wanted to say. Most talked about amusing incidents that happened after school or trips they went on, and sometimes the speaker would bring a prop to make a story more interesting. Fatima knew exactly what she wanted to do.

When her mother came into her room to say goodnight, Fatima set her plan in motion. "Mother, may I please borrow one of your scarves tomorrow? I would like to wear it to school for Talk Time."

Fatima's mother hesitated for a moment, but she knew in her heart that something important was happening. She trusted that Fatima knew what she was doing.

In the morning, Fatima's mother taught her daughter the process of putting on the Hijab.

"No hair should show. When you are old enough, this is a custom you might choose to follow," Fatima's mother said.

"Around your neck and over your head,

and 'round again

until only the brightness of your smiling
face is what is seen by the world."

Fatima dragged herself to the bus stop and waited nervously for the bus to appear. *Maybe it wouldn't come…*but, of course, it did. When Fatima boarded the bus, she felt both different and the same. Everyone was surprised at this dramatic change in their friend.

"What's under the scarf?" Mary asked.

"Did you get a haircut?" Tramel teased, leaning closer to get a good look.

"It's not cold enough for a winter scarf," Alex observed.

"What are you hiding under there?" Mario wanted to know.

Billy sat in the back of the bus, watching Fatima as she found her seat. He said nothing, and Fatima did not look his way.

School days normally passed quickly for Fatima, but this day seemed endless. When Talk Time finally came, she was the first to volunteer. Fatima walked slowly to the front of the classroom. The scarf created a gentle frame around her face—almost forcing her classmates to look into her eyes. Fatima spoke softly, with trembling lips.

"I am Muslim. My religion is called Islam," Fatima stammered as she looked down at the sheet of paper in her hands. "I have been taught that it is important to respect all people."

Fatima felt like she was running out of air. She could barely speak. She glanced down at the paper crumpled in her hands. The words she had so painstakingly printed on notebook paper danced across the page. She inhaled deeply and continued.

"This is my mother's scarf, called a Hijab. When I am old enough, I may choose to wear a Hijab to cover my hair, ears, and neck so other people can really see me. The real me—the me that's inside. My family came to this country to find a better life. The way we dress is a part of our religion, and here we can dress the way that we choose. To me, my mother is the most beautiful woman in the world. She taught me that inside, we are all the same, no matter what we look like on the outside. The Hijab helps people focus on our inner qualities."

Fatima ran out of words. Her mouth went dry. Her classmates stared at her in silence.

"Fatima," her teacher said gently, "is there anything else you would like to add?"

Fatima thought for a moment, and then, without saying anything further, she began to unwrap the Hijab, 'round and 'round under her chin, over her head…until her black hair spilled over her shoulders. The breeze from the open window gently blew a few strands across her sparkling dark eyes.

"I am Fatima," she said. "It's not what I look like, but what I say and then do that matters. Some day, like my mother, I will decide whether I want to wear the Hijab as a part of the way I practice my religion. But no matter what, I'll always be me."

After she finished speaking, there was silence, then her classmates began applauding—all but Billy, who sat quietly, fidgeting with his pencil. Fatima looked at him, but Billy stared at the floor.

Fatima's teacher spoke softly. "Thank you, Fatima. I know that many Muslim women in the world have different ideas about wearing the Hijab. Some are expected to wear the scarf, but it is each individual woman's choice. Fatima has plenty of time to make up her own mind, and one day she'll choose what is right for her. Does anyone have questions or comments about what Fatima has shared?"

Billy looked at his jeans. He studied his red socks, nervously shaking his foot. He was beginning to think maybe he'd made a mistake in making fun of the clothes that other people wear. He analyzed his socks again. He loved those socks, but they were really for a little kid. He still wore them because they reminded him of a fishing trip he once took with his dad.

The bell rang for dismissal, and the students began gathering their things. As everyone headed for the door, Billy edged slowly toward Fatima. Whenever he was nervous, his eyes filled with tears. Billy also had the habit of smiling when he was embarrassed. Teary-eyed and blushing, Billy tossed an apple into the air. After each catch, he rubbed the dirty palm of his hand into his eyes, leaving a smudge below his left eye. Words weren't coming easily. "Is the—the—scarf always the same color?" he stuttered, hoping Fatima wouldn't notice the tears in his eyes.

"Not always," Fatima immediately responded. "Depends. I've seen blue, red, purple, and orange. Some women wear a color to match their clothes. My aunt, Habiba, wears a green scarf that blends with her green eyes."

"Hmmm..." Billy said. "What color do you think...you'd wear?" Billy fumbled his catch, and the apple rolled away.

"Actually, I might also wear green. I want to be a pediatric surgeon like my uncle Abdi. He wears green when he is in the operating room. A green Hijab would match my scrubs! What about you?"

Billy smiled broadly as he showed Fatima his baseball cap. "I like to wear orange and blue. I want to play for New York and pitch the meanest fastball in the major leagues."

He grasped the apple and glanced sideways as if looking at first base. Billy wound his arm like a windmill and threw a perfect strike. His pitch looked so real, Fatima stepped back to watch the make-believe ball scream toward home plate.

His feet planted firmly once again on the sidewalk at the corner of Maple and Edgewood, Billy smiled at the imaginary grandstand where only Fatima stood watching. Coming back to Earth, he polished the apple and took a bite. Then he pulled an orange from his jacket pocket. "You want this?"

"Sure," Fatima replied. "Thank you."

"I'm sorry about what I said…that your mother looks . . ."

"I understand. Thank you. Do you promise you'll never, never, NEVER say anything like that again?" Fatima queried, interrupting Billy.

"I promise," he whispered, rubbing his eyes and gazing at his sneakers.

They climbed onto the school bus together. Billy found a seat beside Mario, and Fatima sat with Mary. Fatima looked at the orange and smiled, relaxing for the first time all day.

When Fatima arrived home, her mother was in the kitchen.

"Fatima, what happened in school today?"

"Nothing." Fatima giggled.

"Nothing?"

"Well, something did," Fatima answered as she inhaled the aroma of the sweet-smelling treats her mother had been baking. "Can we have a snack while I tell you the story?" Placing the Hijab in her mother's hand, Fatima reached up and gave her a joyous hug.